FRANKENSTEIN

Adapted by
Elizabeth Genco

Illustrated by
Jason Ho

Based upon the works of
Mary Shelley

magic wagon

visit us at
www.abdopublishing.com

Published by Magic Wagon, a division of the ABDO Publishing Group, 8000 West 78th Street, Edina, Minnesota 55439.

Printed in the United States of America, North Mankato, Minnesota.
012008 102010
Based upon the works of Mary Shelley
Written by Elizabeth Genco
Illustrated by Jason Ho
Colored & Lettered by Jay Fotos
Edited & Directed by Chazz DeMoss
Cover Design by Neil Klinepier

Library of Congress Cataloging-in-Publication Data

Genco, Elizabeth.
Frankenstein / by Elizabeth Genco ; illustrated by Jason Ho ; based on novel by Mary Shelley.
p. cm. -- (Graphic horror)
ISBN-13: 978-1-60270-059-8
1. Graphic novels. I. Ho, Jason. II. Shelley, Mary Wollstonecraft, 1797-1851. Frankenstein. III. Title.
PN6727.G46F73 2008
741.5'973--dc22

2007016527

"DEAR MARGARET..."
"OUR JOURNEY TO THE NORTH POLE HAS TAKEN A STRANGE AND RATHER DRAMATIC TURN."
"LAST MONDAY WE RAN INTO ICE, WHICH QUICKLY SURROUNDED OUR SHIP ON ALL SIDES."
"THE ICE GOES ON FOR MILES. THE SIGHT WOULD BE A WONDER, DEAR SISTER, IF IT DID NOT PRESENT SUCH A TRIAL."
"BUT THERE WERE OTHER WONDERS."
CAPTAIN WALTON, LOOK!
"OUT ON THE ICE WE FOUND A HALF-FROZEN MAN."
BEFORE I BOARD, I MUST KNOW: WHERE ARE YOU GOING?

"GIVEN THE MAN'S CONDITION, YOU CAN ONLY IMAGINE MY ASTONISHMENT AT THIS QUESTION."
"I ANSWERED AND HE ALLOWED US TO BRING HIM ABOARD."
"HE COLLAPSED INTO BED. WE THOUGHT HE WOULD SURELY DIE."
"HE LIVED."
"IMMEDIATELY UPON WAKING, HE INSISTED UPON TRADING HIS BED FOR THE SHIP'S DECK. HE PACED THERE FOR HOURS, LOOKING OUT TO SEA."
"HE CALLS HIMSELF VICTOR FRANKENSTEIN."
"WHEN ASKED WHY HE CAME TO THIS WRETCHED COLD AND ICE, HIS ANSWER SHOCKED US ALL."
" 'TO FIND THE DEMON - AND DESTROY HIM,' HE SAID."
"FOR DAYS HE SPOKE OF NOTHING ELSE - AND WE FEARED HE HAD GONE MAD."
"BUT OBSESSION AND MADNESS ARE NOT ALWAYS THE SAME, MARGARET. I WAITED FOR HIM TO TELL HIS TALE."
I WAS BORN ABROAD, IN ITALY...

"THE FRANKENSTEIN FAMILY WAS AMONG THE MOST DISTINGUISHED IN ALL GENEVA. OUR NAME GAVE US PRIDE AND EARNED US RESPECT."
"THOUGH MY PARENTS WERE DEVOTED PUBLIC SERVANTS, THEY TRAVELED OFTEN."
"MY MOTHER HAD ESCAPED A LIFE OF POVERTY, AND UNDERSTOOD THE SUFFERING OF THE POOR. VISITING THEM WAS HER CALLING, EVEN WHEN ABROAD."
"ONE SUCH FAMILY HAD 5 MOUTHS TO FEED, INCLUDING A LITTLE GIRL."
"FOR MY MOTHER, IT WAS LOVE AT FIRST SIGHT. SHE LOVED ME WITH ALL HER HEART, BUT HAD ALWAYS WANTED A DAUGHTER, TOO."
"WHEN MY PARENTS PROPOSED AN ADOPTION, BOTH THE COUPLE AND THE PARISH PRIEST READILY AGREED."

"HER NAME WAS ELIZABETH. MY PARENTS KNEW THAT WE WOULD BE CLOSE."

"INDEED, FROM THAT FIRST MOMENT I LOVED HER WITH ALL MY HEART. AND I VOWED TO PROTECT AND CHERISH HER ALWAYS."

"SOON AFTER, MY FAMILY RETURNED TO GENEVA. AND MY BROTHER WILLIAM WAS BORN."

"WHILE MY PARENTS FOCUSED ON THE NEW ARRIVAL, I THREW MYSELF INTO MY STUDIES."
"I HATED CROWDS AND KEPT FEW FRIENDS. INDEED, I HAD ONLY ONE."

"THOUGH MY SERIOUS NATURE HID IT WELL, I ADORED HENRY CLERVAL. HE WAS ALWAYS SO FULL OF LIFE..."

"AS FOR ME, I LONGED FOR LIFE'S SECRETS. I WANTED TO KNOW THE WORKINGS OF NATURE, THE SOUL OF MAN, AND...
...THE SPIRIT OF LIFE ITSELF."

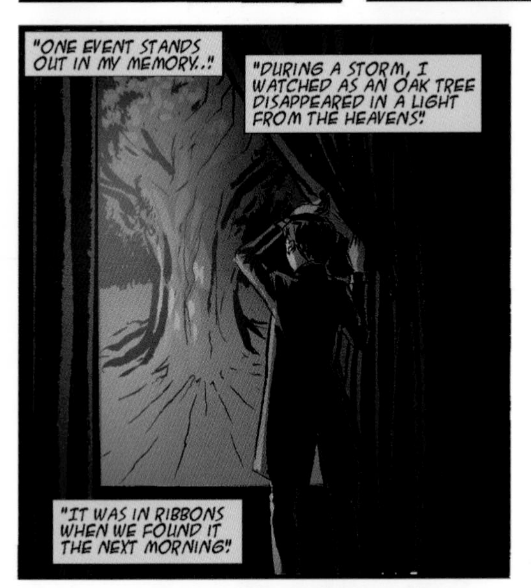
"ONE EVENT STANDS OUT IN MY MEMORY..."
"DURING A STORM, I WATCHED AS AN OAK TREE DISAPPEARED IN A LIGHT FROM THE HEAVENS."
"IT WAS IN RIBBONS WHEN WE FOUND IT THE NEXT MORNING."

"WHEN I LEARNED WHAT A POWERFUL FORCE THE LIGHTNING WAS, I KNEW THAT SCIENCE WAS MY FUTURE."

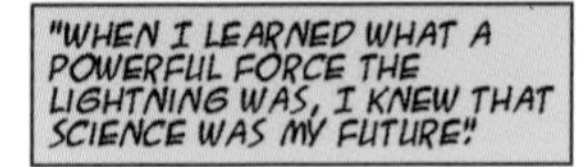
"I HAD TO UNDERSTAND THE MYSTERIES OF LIFE... AND DEATH. OF CREATION AND DESTRUCTION."

"WHEN I WAS 17, ELIZABETH FELL ILL WITH SCARLET FEVER. YOUTH GAVE HER THE STRENGTH TO FIGHT, AND SHE RECOVERED FULLY."
"MY MOTHER, HER CARETAKER, DID NOT."
"IN HER FINAL MOMENTS, MOTHER GAVE US HER LAST WISHES."
YOUR UNION BEGAN LONG AGO, VICTOR AND ELIZABETH. MY CHILDREN, YOU MUST GET MARRIED.
"AND SO OUR FATES WERE INDEED SEALED. IT WAS OUR MOTHER'S LAST WISH."
"SHE GAVE US A GIFT BY SAYING WHAT WE HAD LEFT UNSPOKEN FOR YEARS."
"NOT LONG AFTER HER DEATH, I LEFT FOR SCHOOL AT INGOLSTADT."
"THERE, I MET TWO PROFESSORS WHO CHANGED THE COURSE OF MY STUDIES AND MY DESTINY..."
IN THIS DAY AND AGE, VICTOR, I HARDLY EXPECTED TO FIND YOU FILLING YOUR HEAD WITH SUPERSTITION INSTEAD OF SCIENCE.
YOU MUST BEGIN AGAIN!
"PROFESSOR KREMPE PLACED ME IN THE ABLE HANDS OF PROFESSOR WALDMAN."
CHEMISTRY IS THE BASIS FOR ALL THAT WE SEE AND FEEL. WITH CHEMISTRY, WE SHALL SOON UNDERSTAND LIFE ITSELF!
"AS HE SPOKE, ONE PURPOSE GRIPPED MY HEART."
"I WILL DISCOVER THE SECRET OF LIFE. I WILL DISCOVER HOW TO CREATE IT."

"I APPROACHED WALDMAN IN HIS LABORATORY AND ASKED HIM FOR ADVICE.."
MY BOY, OF COURSE YOU MAY USE MY BOOKS AND MY TOOLS. I WOULD BE HONORED TO HELP YOU.
"UNDER HIS CARE, I BUILT MY OWN LAB AND A SOLID BODY OF KNOWLEDGE."
"I BECAME OBSESSED. MONTHS, THEN YEARS PASSED AS I DEVOTED EVERY FIBER IN MY BEING TO THE ART.."
"TO FINDING THE SECRETS OF GIVING THE SPARK OF LIFE TO AN EMPTY SHELL... THE SECRET OF CREATION.."
"THESE WERE THE REWARDS OF MY LABORS!"
"I DECIDED TO CREATE A MAN. I WOULD GIVE HIM LIFE, JUST LIKE A FATHER."
"AND LIKE A FATHER, I WOULD RECEIVE HIS GRATITUDE COMPLETELY."
"I WORKED WITHOUT REST FOR MANY MONTHS. AND ON A DREARY NIGHT IN NOVEMBER, IT WAS TIME.."
"AS I PREPARED FOR THE EXPERIMENT, MY ANTICIPATION TURNED TO AGONY."
"IT HAD BEEN MORE THAN TWO YEARS SINCE I BEGAN, I WAS CRAZED, EXHAUSTED.. MY CANDLE NEARLY BURNED OUT.."

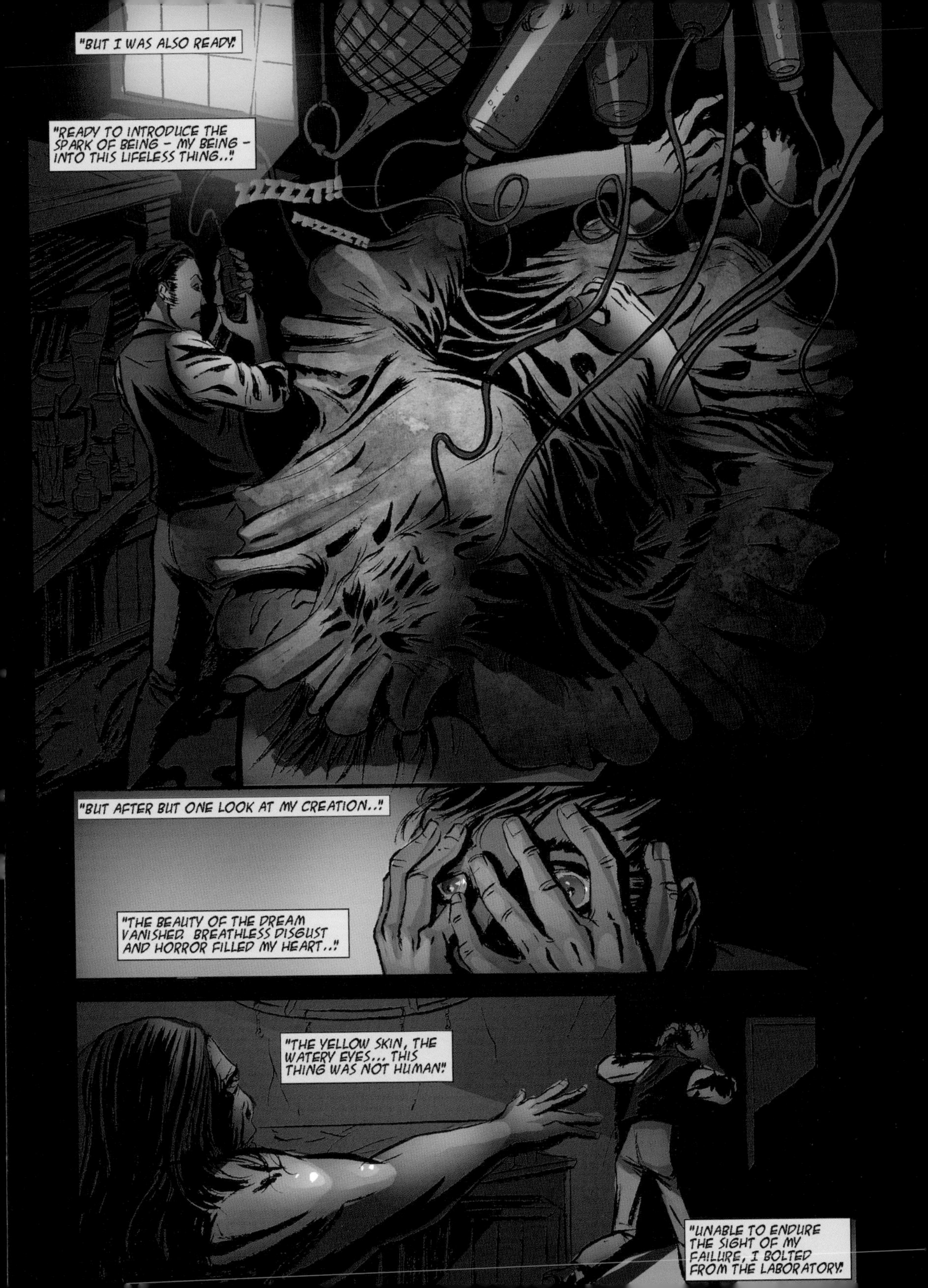
"BUT I WAS ALSO READY."
"READY TO INTRODUCE THE SPARK OF BEING - MY BEING - INTO THIS LIFELESS THING..."
ZZZZZZT!!
"BUT AFTER BUT ONE LOOK AT MY CREATION..."
"THE BEAUTY OF THE DREAM VANISHED. BREATHLESS DISGUST AND HORROR FILLED MY HEART..."
"THE YELLOW SKIN, THE WATERY EYES... THIS THING WAS NOT HUMAN."
"UNABLE TO ENDURE THE SIGHT OF MY FAILURE, I BOLTED FROM THE LABORATORY."

"MORNING CAME, AND I FRANTICALLY SOUGHT REFUGE ON THE STREETS OF INGOLSTADT."
"FEAR GRIPPED ME AS I WALKED. MAYBE THE HORRID THING HAD FOLLOWED ME..."
"IT HAD NOT. INSTEAD, A RANDOM MEETING WITH HENRY WAS MY SALVATION."
VICTOR! WHAT HAS HAPPENED, DEAR FRIEND?
DO NOT ASK, DO NOT SPEAK OF IT... OH, I CANNOT BEAR IT...
"HENRY TOOK ME BACK TO HIS APARTMENT."
VICTOR! WHAT IN GOD'S NAME IS THE MATTER?
DO NOT ASK ME. HE CAN TELL. SAVE ME!
"IT WAS THE BEGINNING OF A FEVER THAT WOULD LAST FOR MONTHS."
"HENRY ACCEPTED MY SILENCE WILLINGLY, AND LOOKED AFTER ME LIKE I WAS HIS OWN SON."
"OH, I DID NOT DESERVE THIS."
"AS I GREW STRONGER, I PUT THE MONSTER OUT OF MY MIND."
"AND ALL THE WHILE, I SECRETLY PRAYED THAT THE HORROR WAS BEHIND ME."

"A LETTER FROM MY FATHER PROVED OTHERWISE."
"'HOW CAN I SPEAK OF SUCH HORRIBLE NEWS?' HE WROTE."
"'WILLIAM, YOUR SWEET BROTHER, IS DEAD. VICTOR, HE IS MURDERED!' HE WROTE."
"THE PRINT OF THE MURDERER'S FINGER WAS ON HIS NECK."
"I RESOLVED TO VISIT THE VERY SPOT WHERE POOR WILLIAM HAD FALLEN. I LEFT FOR GENEVA AT ONCE."
"THE CITY GATES WERE CLOSED BY THEN, LEAVING ME STRANDED IN THE MIDDLE OF A STORM."
"THE WRETCH WAS THERE! THE FILTHY DEMON TO WHOM I HAD GIVEN LIFE! WHEN I SAW HIM, I KNEW THE TRUTH."
"HE WAS THE MURDERER! THERE WAS NO DOUBT."
"BUT A PICTURE LAST SEEN IN WILLIAM'S POSSESSION, WAS FOUND ON JUSTINE, A GIRL KEEPING ELIZABETH COMPANY IN MY ABSENCE."
"FLIMSY AS IT WAS, THE EVIDENCE WAS IMPOSSIBLE TO ARGUE. JUSTINE WAS PUNISHED FOR THE MURDER."

"AFTER THE EXECUTION, MY SADNESS ONLY GREW WORSE. FINALLY MY FATHER SUGGESTED A TRIP TO THE FAMILY HOME."
"I TOOK TO THE MOUNTAINS, HOPING THE CLEAR AIR WOULD LIFT MY SPIRITS..."
"BUT I WAS TO FIND NO PEACE."
"HOW HAD HE FOLLOWED ME HERE? TRULY, I AM CURSED!"
DEVIL! HOW DARE YOU!
DO YOU NOT FEAR MY PUNISHMENT?
IF ONLY I COULD BRING YOUR VICTIMS BACK TO LIFE BY ENDING YOUR MISERABLE EXISTENCE!
HEAR ME OUT BEFORE YOU VENT YOUR HATRED. YOU MADE ME! I WILL BE GENTLE IF YOU TREAT ME SO.
NO! I WILL NOT GIVE AUDIENCE TO A VILLAIN.
LISTEN!
FRANKENSTEIN, I ASK YOU NOT TO SPARE ME, BUT ONLY TO LISTEN. ONLY THEN, IF YOU MUST, DESTROY ME, THE WORK OF YOUR OWN HANDS.
HEAR MY STORY, AND DECIDE MY FATE.
HE LEAD ME TO A CAVE OF ICE TO BEGIN HIS TALE.

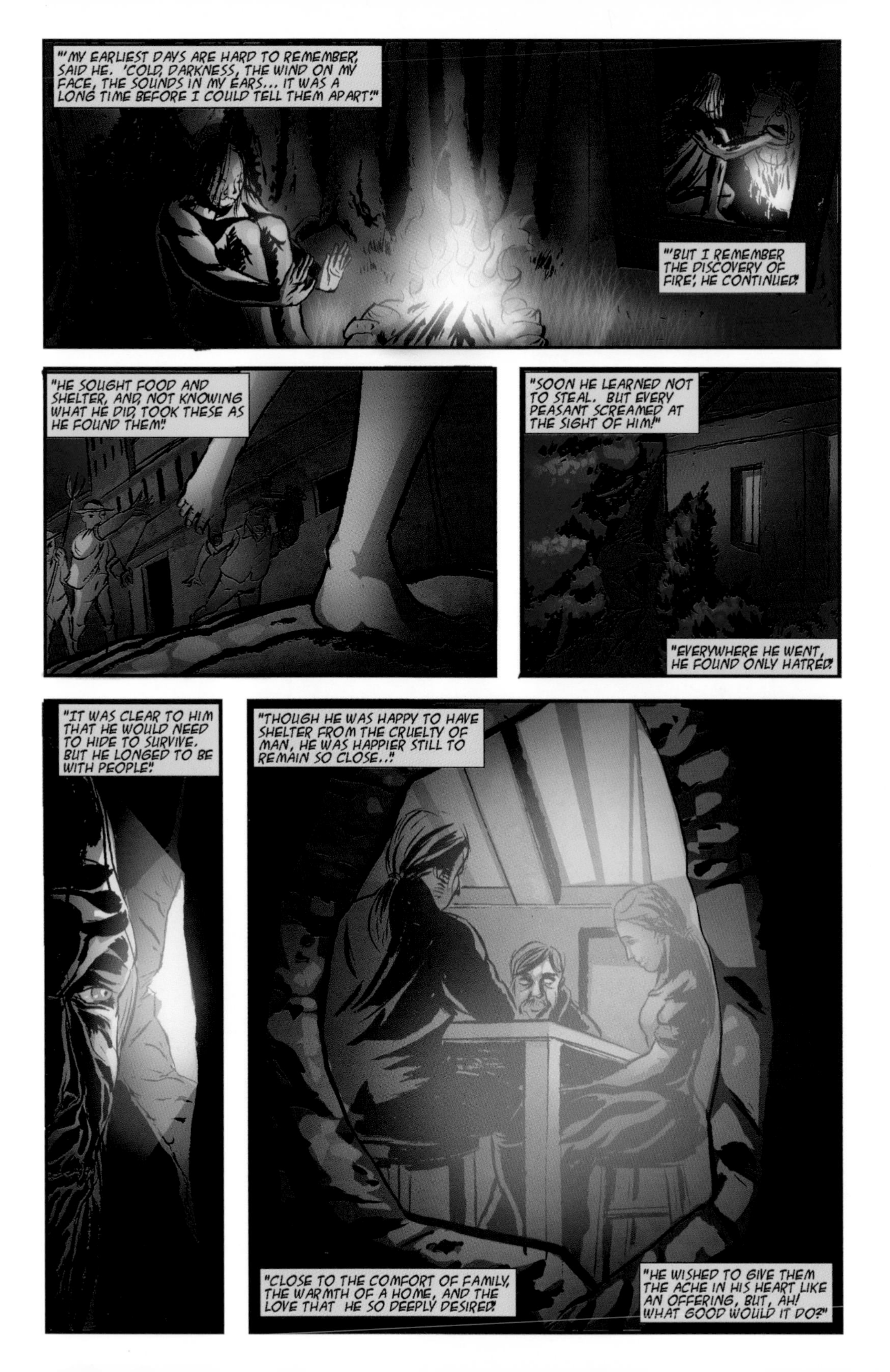
"'My earliest days are hard to remember,' said he. 'Cold, darkness, the wind on my face, the sounds in my ears... it was a long time before I could tell them apart.'"
"'But I remember the discovery of fire,' he continued."
"He sought food and shelter, and, not knowing what he did, took these as he found them."
"Soon he learned not to steal. But every peasant screamed at the sight of him."
"Everywhere he went, he found only hatred."
"It was clear to him that he would need to hide to survive. But he longed to be with people."
"Though he was happy to have shelter from the cruelty of man, he was happier still to remain so close..."
"Close to the comfort of family, the warmth of a home, and the love that he so deeply desired."
"He wished to give them the ache in his heart like an offering, but, ah! What good would it do?"

"HE APPLIED HIS TALENTS TO A MORE MUNDANE TASK."
"BY CHANCE, HE CAUGHT SIGHT OF HIS REFLECTION IN A POOL OF WATER."
"AT FIRST, HE COULD SCARCELY BELIEVE THAT HE WAS THAT CREATURE. LONG HAD HE ADMIRED THE PERFECT FORMS OF THE COTTAGERS."
" BUT THERE IS NO HIDING FROM THE MONSTER THAT HE IS."
"WHILE HE COULD NOT SHED HIS GHASTLY SHELL, PERHAPS HE COULD OVERCOME IT WITH ACTS OF KINDNESS. AND PERHAPS THESE ACTS SHOULD TOUCH OTHERS."
FELIX, LOOK! COME QUICKLY!
"THIS WAS HIS ONLY SATISFACTION. HIS ONLY REWARD."
IT IS ENOUGH TO LAST US FOR SEVERAL DAYS! WHERE DID IT COME FROM?
I-IT... IT IS... EENUF...
"HE WAS DETERMINED TO REACH THEM. AND FOR THAT, HE WOULD NEED THEIR LANGUAGE."
"IT WAS DIFFICULT AT FIRST. BUT THEN HE HAPPENED ON A SATCHEL OF BOOKS. HE LEARNED STEADILY."
"SOON, IT WAS TIME TO COME OUT OF HIDING."

"MY MONSTER CONTINUED HIS STORY, 'THE BLIND MAN AND I CONNECTED IMMEDIATELY. HIS FONDNESS FOR ME GREW AS WE AWAITED THE ARRIVAL OF HIS TWO CHILDREN'."
"'SURELY, HE WOULD HELP THEM UNDERSTAND. HELP THEM SEE! HE THOUGHT'."
"BUT THEY WERE MORE BLIND THAN HE".
MISERABLE WRETCH! GET OUT! GET OUT!
"'YOU CALL ME A MURDERER, BUT, YOU MUST KNOW THE TRUTH', HE TOLD THEM".
"HE TRIED SO HARD TO HELP HUMANS".
"NOTHING COULD SOFTEN THEIR HARD, HARD HEARTS".
"A HEART OF STONE CLAMORS FOR ONE THING: REVENGE".
"SOON HIS OWN HEART BEGAN TO TURN... TO CALCIFY..."
"HE TOLD ME, 'YOUR BROTHER'S PREJUDICE SEALED HIS FATE, AND MINE'."
CALM YOURSELF, CHILD. I SHALL NOT HURT YOU.
LET ME GO! MY FATHER IS M. FRANKENSTEIN - LET ME GO OR HE WILL PUNISH YOU!
"HE LEFT HIM NO CHOICE".

"AFTER IT WAS DONE, HE FOUND A LOCKET ON MY BROTHER'S BREAST. THE WOMAN IN IT WAS THE MOST BEAUTIFUL CREATURE HE HAD EVER SEEN."
"A CREATURE HE COULD NEVER HAVE."
"IN A NEARBY BARN, HE SAW A WOMAN YET FAIRER STILL. HE IMAGINED HER SMILE, WHAT JOY IT MUST BRING... BUT NOT FOR HIM. NEVER FOR HIM!"
"IF SHE WERE TO SEE HIM, SURELY SHE WOULD CURSE HIM. CALL HIM A MURDERER..."
"IT IS AS IT HAS ALWAYS BEEN."
"AFTER HE FINISHED TELLING HIS TALE, HE TURNED TO ME."
FOR SOME DAYS, I HAVE HAUNTED THIS SPOT. I HAVE BEEN CONSUMED BY RAGE AND PASSION THAT ONLY YOU CAN SATISFY. YOU SHALL DIE HERE NOW UNLESS YOU MAKE ME A PROMISE.
MAN WILL NOT HAVE ME. BUT SOMEONE AS DEFORMED AND HORRIBLE AS I - SHE WILL. YOU MUST CREATE HER FOR ME AS YOU HAVE MADE ME.
YOU HAVE NO RIGHT TO REFUSE.
"HORRID! YET, I KNEW HE WAS RIGHT. I COULD NOT REFUSE."
IF I DO THIS, YOU MUST SWEAR, TOO. SWEAR THAT IT ENDS THEN.
I SWEAR, BY THE SUN AND HEAVEN, AND BY THE FIRE THAT STILL BURNS IN MY HEART. IF YOU MAKE ME A MATE, NO MAN SHALL EVER SEE ME AGAIN.
IT WAS DONE.

"AND SO IT BEGAN. MY FATHER WISHED FOR ME TO MARRY SWEET ELIZABETH, BUT I WAS DETERMINED TO PUT AN END TO MY SLAVERY. ONCE AGAIN, I SECLUDED MYSELF!
"AS I WORKED, I COULDN'T HELP BUT REFLECT..."
"THREE YEARS AGO, I HAD CREATED THIS FIEND. HE HAS BROUGHT NOTHING BUT DEATH, SUFFERING AND MADNESS INTO THIS WORLD!
"I NOW MAKE ANOTHER, NOW KNOWING HOW SHE WOULD BEHAVE!
"HE SAID HIS ACTS WERE REVENGE, BUT WHAT IF SHE MURDERED FOR ITS OWN SAKE?"
"HE HAD SWORN TO HIDE, BUT SHE HAS NOT..."
"WHAT IF THEY HATE EACH OTHER?"
"WHAT IF THEY HAVE CHILDREN?"
"THIS IS MADNESS!"
GRRAAHHH!!!

SLAVE! YOU THINK YOU ARE MISERABLE? I CAN MAKE YOU HATE THE VERY LIGHT OF DAY!
UNDERSTAND THAT YOU ARE MY CREATOR, BUT I AM NOW YOUR MASTER.
SHALL EACH BEAST HAVE HIS MATE AND I BE ALONE? ARE YOU TO BE HAPPY WHILE I GROVEL?
REMEMBER MY STONE HEART REMAINS. BEWARE, FOR I AM FEARLESS -
AND I SHALL BE WITH YOU ON YOUR WEDDING NIGHT.
"HIS WORDS RANG IN MY EARS LONG AFTER ALL WAS SILENT..."
"IMAGES OF MY OLD LIFE - MY FATHER, CLERVAL, MY BRIDE-TO-BE - SWIRLED IN THE DARKNESS. I RESOLVED TO QUIT THIS HORRID BUSINESS FOR GOOD."
"BUT THERE WAS ONE MORE TASK TO PERFORM."
"I WISH I COULD SAY THAT IT LIFTED MY BURDENS, BUT..."
"... FAR GREATER HORRORS AWAITED ME ONSHORE."

COME, SIR – YOU MUST GIVE AN ACCOUNT OF YOURSELF BEFORE MR. KIRWAN, THE MAGISTRATE.
BUT WHY?
"THEY HAD FOUND A BODY ON THE SHORE... AND I HAD BEEN THE ONLY MAN IN SIGHT."
"A WOMAN WAITING FOR HER FISHERMAN TO RETURN SAID SHE SAW MY BOAT PUSH OFF SHORTLY BEFORE THE BODY WAS FOUND."
"THE BODY WAS NOT YET COLD WHEN THEY BROUGHT IT IN."
"THERE WAS NO SIGN OF VIOLENCE, SAVE FOR THE BLACK FINGER MARKS AT THE NECK."
"THE MOMENT THAT THEY PULLED BACK THE SHEET REMAINS A NIGHTMARE FROM WHICH I SWEAR I SHALL NEVER WAKE. MY DEAR FRIEND HENRY WAS UNDERNEATH."
"WHY DID I NOT DIE?"
"WAS I NOT A MURDERER MYSELF?"

"WHY WAS I DOOMED TO LIVE?"
"I WAS NOT INNOCENT OF THEIR CHARGES. WILLIAM, JUSTINE, HENRY... ALL DIED BY MY HANDS!"

"A JAIL CELL WAS BUT A SLIGHT PUNISHMENT FOR MY CRIMES!"
WHOSE MURDER AM I RESPONSIBLE FOR THIS TIME?
FEAR NOT, SIR. YOUR FAMILY IS PERFECTLY WELL.
AND A FRIEND HAS COME TO VISIT YOU.?
FATHER!!

I'VE COME TO TAKE YOU HOME, SON. THEY HAVE NO EVIDENCE - THEY CANNOT HOLD YOU.

"WE SET SAIL FOR GENEVA SOON AFTER. BUT I KNEW THERE WOULD BE NO PEACE. AND I HAD BUT ONE JOB TO DO!"
"TO WATCH OVER MY LOVED ONES, LAY IN WAIT FOR THE MURDERER... AND PUT AN END TO HIM!"

"I WOULD NOT SLEEP. I WOULD NOT REST!"

GENEVA, MONTHS LATER.
"MY WEDDING TO ELIZABETH SHOULD HAVE BEEN A HAPPY TIME. BUT IT WAS FILLED WITH DREAD FOR WHAT WAS TO COME."
"THE MONSTER HAD MADE A PROMISE. HE WOULD KEEP IT."
"I TOOK EVERY PRECAUTION. I SENT MEN TO SURROUND THE FAMILY HOME, KEPT WEAPONS IN THE BRIDAL SUITE... AND DIDN'T TELL ELIZABETH A THING."
"AND WHEN THE CEREMONY WAS DONE..."
"...ALL THAT WAS LEFT TO DO WAS WAIT."
VICTOR, WHAT'S WRONG? THERE IS NO SENSE IN HIDING YOUR DISTRESS. I SEE IT PLAINLY...
DO NOT ASK ME THESE THINGS, ELIZABETH.
IT'S TIME FOR BED NOW.
YES. GO TO OUR ROOM AND LOCK THE DOOR.
BUT VICTOR -
DO NOT OPEN IT, FOR ANYONE. NO MATTER WHAT.
"I HATED TO DISAPPOINT HER ON OUR WEDDING NIGHT."
"BUT SHE MUST NOT SEE WHAT IS COMING."
COME AND GET ME, FIEND. IT IS TIME TO KEEP YOUR WORD. AND IN TURN, I SHALL MAKE GOOD ON MINE.
IT ENDS HERE.
AIEeEEE!
"INDEED, IT DID."

"AND THAT IS WHEN I FINALLY UNDERSTOOD THE DEPTHS OF MY SELF-DECEPTION..."
"THE MONSTER'S WEDDING NIGHT VISIT WAS NEVER MEANT FOR ME."
"HE MOUTHED WORDS THROUGH THE WINDOW. 'AND NOW WE ARE EVEN!'"
"A STONE HEART FOR A STONE HEART."
"AH, BUT HE UNDERESTIMATED ME."
"I WOULD MATCH HIS RAGE, HIS THIRST FOR REVENGE!"
"AT THAT MOMENT, WE WERE EVEN."

"THE DEATH OF ELIZABETH WAS TOO MUCH FOR MY FATHER'S ALREADY FRAIL HEALTH."
"BUT I HAD BECOME NUMB TO DEATH."
"A HEART OF STONE DOES NOT FEEL."
"I WOULD BEGIN A JOURNEY. AND I WOULD NEED THE HELP OF MY VICTIMS. I VISITED THEM ONE LAST TIME."
BY THIS SACRED EARTH ON WHICH I DO KNEEL, HERE I DO SWEAR...
ELIZABETH LAVENZA FRANKENSTEIN WIFE DAUGHTER
M. FRANKENSTEIN FATHER HUSBAND
TO PURSUE YOUR MURDERER TO THE ENDS OF THE EARTH, UNTIL HE IS DESTROYED.
AND I CALL ON YOU, SPIRITS OF THE DEAD, TO AID ME IN THIS WORK.
HA HAH HA HA
A NOBLE AIM, CREATOR. ALAS, YOU SEEM DETERMINED TO LIVE...
FOR AS LONG AS YOU DO, THEY SHALL REMAIN UN-AVENGED.
NO!!
"I VOWED NOT TO REST UNTIL IT IS DONE. I SHALL FOLLOW HIM TO THE ENDS OF THE EARTH."

"THE PURSUED SHALL BECOME THE PURSUER."
"AND HE SHALL KNOW NO PEACE."

"LET HIM THINK THAT HE IS BETTER THAN ME, HIS MAKER. LET HIM THINK HE CAN HIDE FROM ME."
"FOR I KNOW BETTER.."

"THE BOAT HEADED NORTH, INTO THE ICE. A PLACE NOT FIT FOR MEN OF THIS EARTH. IT SEEMED FITTING THAT IT SHOULD END THERE."
"I MADE THE PREPARATIONS."

"HE LEFT HORROR WHEREVER HE WENT. LITTLE DID HE KNOW HOW EASY HE WAS TO FOLLOW."
"EACH TRACE OF HIM MADDENINGLY SPURRED ME ON TO THE NEXT.."

"IT WAS ONLY A MATTER OF TIME."

WILLIAM! JUSTINE! HENRY! FATHER!
ELIZABETH...!
IT WILL NOT BE LONG NOW. I PROMISE YOU.

KEEP ON!
"I GOT SO CLOSE..."
CRAAACK!
SWEAR HE SHALL NOT LIVE...

"AT THE END OF HIS STORY, DEAR MARGARET, THE MAN WAS WEAKER THAN EVER."
SWEAR THAT YOU WILL KEEP GOING. YOU MUST. IT IS IN YOUR HANDS NOW...

HE MUST NOT LIVE...
"THE CREWMEN ARE ANGRY. THEY HAVE NO PATIENCE FOR A MADMAN'S RAVINGS."
"BUT HOW COULD I FEEL ANYTHING BUT PITY FOR A MAN WHO CHASES A GHOST? A PHANTOM?"

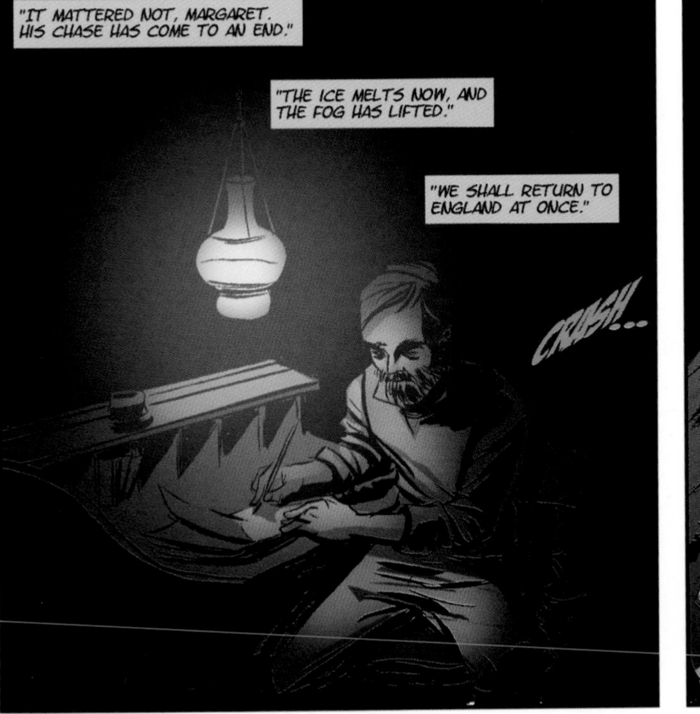
"IT MATTERED NOT, MARGARET. HIS CHASE HAS COME TO AN END."
"THE ICE MELTS NOW, AND THE FOG HAS LIFTED."
"WE SHALL RETURN TO ENGLAND AT ONCE."
CRASH...

BOOOM
WHAT? WHO IS THERE?

AH, CREATOR. AH, FATHER!
SO LONG I HAVE DWELLED IN DARKNESS. ONLY NOW DO I SEE THE LIGHT OF DAY.
ONLY NOW... WHEN YOUR HEART IS STILL.
WHAT IS THIS MADNESS?
WHAT HAVE I DONE?

YOU!
WHY HAVE YOU COME?
BETTER THAT YOU REMAIN A PHANTOM. YOUR HORRIBLE WORK IS DONE!
IT IS TRUE! BUT I BEG YOU - FIND KINDNESS IN YOUR HEART. HAVE PITY!
FOR MAN IS MY FATHER. AND ALL I WANT - ALL I HAVE EVER WANTED - IS HIS LOVE.
WITHOUT LOVE, THERE IS SUFFERING. AND YOUR HATRED TOWARD ME CANNOT EQUAL THAT WHICH I HAVE FOR MYSELF.
YOUR WHINING HAS NO EFFECT ON ME. YOU HAD YOUR CHANCE TO MAKE RIGHT.
INSTEAD, YOU LET THE DEMON WITHIN TAKE YOU.
QUIT HERE NOW, OR I SHALL UNLEASH MINE.
SIR, SAVE YOUR ENERGY. I DO NOT NEED YOUR THREATS. DO NOT LET THE STONE SEEP INTO YOUR HEART AS IT DID MINE AND MY FATHER'S.
I WILL GLADLY TAKE MY LEAVE, FOR THERE IS ONLY ONE PLACE FOR ME NOW.

I SHALL GO TO THE FUNERAL PYRE. AND I SHALL LIGHT IT BY MY OWN HAND.
AND WHEN MY BODY HAS TURNED TO ASHES...
THE WIND SHALL SWEEP THEM INTO THE SEA.

Mary Wollstonecraft Godwin

Mary Wollstonecraft Godwin was born in London, England, on August 30, 1797. She was the only child of William Godwin and Mary Wollstonecraft. Both of her parents were writers. Her mother died soon after her birth and her father raised her.

Mary never had a formal education, though she did learn to read. She read at home from her father's extensive library. She also wrote her own stories in her spare time.

In 1812, Mary met author Percy Bysshe Shelley and his wife Harriet. During the next couple of years, the three spent a lot of time together. Mary and Percy soon fell in love, and in 1814 they eloped to France. They were married two years later after Harriet passed away. Mary and Percy had a son, Percy Florence Shelley.

During their marriage, the Shelleys traveled and continued to write. Mary wrote her best-known work, Frankenstein, in 1818. In 1822, Percy Shelley died. Mary and her son returned to London, where Mary continued to write. On February 1, 1851, Mary Shelley died in London.

Mary Shelley Has Many Additional Works Including

Mathilda (1819)
Valperga (1823)
The Last Man (1826)
The Fortunes of Perkin Warbeck (1830)
Lodore (1835)
Falkner (1837)

Glossary

anticipation - the act of looking forward to an event or receiving an object.

dramatic - having a striking effect.

execution - the act of putting a person to death according to law.

obsession - a continued, disturbing need to think about an object, idea, or feeling.

pyre - a heap of material used to burn a body in a funeral ceremony.

salvation - a person or place that saves a person from destruction or failure.

Web Sites

To learn more about Mary Shelley, visit ABDO Publishing Company on the World Wide Web at **www.abdopublishing.com**. Web sites about Shelley are featured on our Book Links page. These links are routinely monitored and updated to provide the most current information available.